WHO DO
YOU MISS
RIGHT
NOW?

WHAT SONG
DO YOU KNOW
BY HEART?

DO YOU
LIKE YOUR
NAME?

HELLO WORLD!

BY
Kelly Corrigan

ILLUSTRATED BY
Stacy Ebert

FLAMINGO BOOKS

It's happening.

You're moving on.

The beginning

Who knows what you'll find out there?

Maybe buildings with banners.
Or balconies with birdcages.

There could be bases, bats, and balls.

Or benches, blankets, and barbecues.

There might even be bobsledding!

No matter where you go,

there is one thing you will always find . . .

People!

People will be everywhere!

People with braids.

People with beards.

People with burkas,

and big, tall buns.

People in ballgowns.

People in blue jeans.

People with black belts,

and one or two in bell bottoms.

There will be boys who belch.

And some girls too.

There will be people
chasing butterflies,
and bystanders just being.

Ballerinas on bicycles.

Bucktoothed girls and bashful boys.

Bullies who bully.

Bossy busdrivers
and people who brag.

But here's the thing . . .
There's more to the
belchers and the bashful
and the bystanders
than you think.

There's more to everyone than you think.

So how will you know?

What do you want? And why do you want it?

Who do you miss? And what makes you miss them?

Who do you love? And what makes you love them?

You'll become the best question-asker the world has ever seen!

WORLD'S BEST
QUESTION-ASKER

That's how you'll find out that the butterfly-chaser
knows how to swim backstroke.

And the bucktoothed girl wishes for braces.

The ballerina misses her grandpa Benny.

And the bashful boy loves his basset hound.

The bystander bakes the
best banana bread in town.

The girl who burps
wants to start a
burp-bottling business.

And the bully was bullied.

That's how he learned to do it.

You'll say,

"How do you make your bun
so big and tall?"

"What do you do after you catch a butterfly?"

"Did you ever back up into a bush or get busted for speeding?"

And the things they will tell you!

Oh, the things they will tell you.

Surprising things,
scary things,
and some very silly things.

Oh, the people you will know!

People who will make you sigh and cry,

cheer and wonder,

think and rethink!

People who will make you
smarter and stronger,
steadier and softer,

better and bigger hearted . . .

and even more beloved than you have always been.

FLAMINGO BOOKS

An imprint of Penguin Random House LLC, New York

First published in the United States of America by Flamingo Books,
an imprint of Penguin Random House LLC, 2021

Text copyright © 2021 by Kelly Corrigan
Illustrations copyright © 2021 by Stacy Ebert

Flamingo Books & colophon are registered trademarks of Penguin Random House LLC.

Visit us online at penguinrandomhouse.com.

Library of Congress Cataloging-in-Publication Data is available.

Printed in the United States of America • Text set in Oxtail

ISBN 9780593206065

10 9 8 7 6 5 4 3 2 1

The art for this book was rendered in pencil, and finished in Photoshop with a Wacom tablet.

WHAT MAKES SOMEONE SMART?

WHAT DOES LOVE FEEL LIKE?

HAVE YOU EVER BEEN TO THE HOSPITAL?

IF YOU HAD A STORE, WHAT WOULD IT SELL?